The Three Donalds

a tartan fantasy

dedicated to Knightsbridge Nursery School, Livingston

Published in 1998 by
SCOTTISH CHILDREN'S PRESS
Unit 14, Leith Walk Business Centre,
130 Leith Walk, Edinburgh EH6 5DT
Tel: 0131 555 5950 • Fax: 0131 555 5018
e-mail: scp@sol.co.uk
http://www.taynet.co.uk/users/scp

Scottish Children's Press is an imprint of Scottish Cultural Press

British Library Cataloguing in Publication Data
A catalogue record for this book is available from the British Library

The publisher acknowledges subsidy from the Scottish Arts Council
towards the publication of this volume

ISBN: 1 899827 60 9

Printed and bound by Interprint Ltd, Malta

The Three Donalds

a tartan fantasy

Linda Bandelier
and David Campbell

illustrated by Ian Shields

SCOTTISH CHILDREN'S PRESS

This story happened a long time ago in Scotland . . . long before you were born, long before I was born, long before your mothers, your fathers or your grannies and grandpas were born. It was a *long* time ago. It happened up in the Highlands, in a little village, and that village was in a beautiful green glen.

Now, if you went up the glen, you went to the east. And there at the top of the glen were tree-covered mountains, and in the morning the sun burst above them with its red and pink and gold sunrises. And if you went down the glen, you went to the west. And there at the foot of the glen was a pebble beach with a beautiful, beautiful blue sea where the sun set in the evening in red and pink and gold sunsets.

Now the village was filled with excitement.

Everyone knew that three young couples – the MacCraes, the MacLennans and the MacLeods – were all expecting babies! And they were astonished when all three babies arrived on the very same day! Their astonishment turned to wonder when they discovered that all three had been born at the very same hour!

Well, it wasn't long before a group of villagers got together with the fiddler, a bottle of whisky, some bannocks and some gifts for the babies. Off they went to hansel them, to welcome and offer them a blessing for their lives.

So, following the merry steps of the fiddler, they climbed first to the top of the hill where the cottage of the MacCraes was perched. There they knocked on the door.

The proud father opened it at once and said, 'Welcome! Welcome! Come in, meet our new son!'

'Isn't that lovely – a baby boy born to the MacCraes! And what are you going to call him?'

'Donald. His name is Donald.'

'Oh, that's a fine name, a fine-sounding name: Donald MacCrae. Just look – he's got a head full of hair!'

They gazed in astonishment for indeed he had a whole shock of hair! It wasn't black, it wasn't brown and it wasn't blond. It was red – bright red hair! And his eyes, they were very unusual. They weren't blue and they weren't green. They were brown – sparkling brown eyes!

'Oh, what a handsome son you have.' And the fiddler played a merry tune, and they drank to the health of Donald MacCrae.

'This is an amazing morning. We've two more calls to make so we'll have to be on our way.'

So the villagers bade farewell to the MacCraes and off they went, down the hill and up the glen to the snug little cottage of the MacLennans. They knocked on the door.

When it opened, there stood the proud father.

'Welcome!' he said. 'Welcome! Come in and meet our new son!'

'Oh,' said the villagers, 'a boy, another baby boy! And what are you going to call him?'

'Donald,' said the couple.

'Donald!' said the villagers in surprise. 'Donald! Imagine, two baby Donalds born on the same day, at the same hour, in our village. The MacCrae's little one is called "Donald" too, you know.'

'Och, he'll be nothing like ours – just wait till you see him!'

And there he was, with a head full of hair. It wasn't black, it wasn't brown and it wasn't blond. It was red – bright red hair!

'Just look at his eyes!'

His eyes were most unusual. They weren't blue, they weren't green – they were brown, sparkling brown eyes.

'What a handsome little fellow he is! And what a fine-sounding name: Donald MacLennan!'

With that the fiddler began a beautiful, merry tune and they drank to the health of Donald MacLennan.

'Now, we've one more call to make. We'll need to be on our way.'

So the villagers bade farewell to the MacLennans and they went down the glen, all the way down to the shore to the sea-sprayed cottage of the MacLeods.

'Welcome! Welcome!' said proud Mr MacLeod. 'Come in and meet our new son!'

'A *third* baby boy! What a strange thing! And what are you going to call him?'

The couple smiled and said, 'Donald. His name is Donald.'

'Donald! Imagine that,' said the villagers. 'Three baby boys – *three* baby Donalds – all born in our village on the *same* day at the *same* hour.

'You know, the strange thing is that the MacCraes and the MacLennans also have little boys and they're both called Donald as well.'

'Och, they'll be nothing like ours – just wait till you see him!'

There he was, with a shock of hair. It wasn't black, it

wasn't brown and it wasn't blond. It was red – bright red hair!

'Just look at his eyes!' said one of the villagers.

His eyes were most unusual. They weren't blue, they weren't green – they were brown, sparkling brown eyes.

'Oh, baby Donald MacLeod is a fine, handsome fellow,' said the villagers. So they drank to the health of Donald MacLeod while the fiddler played a merry tune.

At last, they bade farewell to the MacLeods and made their way home.

Of course, it wasn't long before the proud parents wanted to show one another their babies. So they wrapped their three red-headed Donalds in three white shawls and they all set out.

Under the old, green rowan tree they met, for it was a great gathering place for the villagers. There they laid the three babies, the three Donalds, side by side on the ground. But not for long . . . for when they looked from one to the other, to the other . . . they could not tell them apart!

So Mrs MacCrae at once snatched up her Donald and held him close. And Mrs MacLennan snatched up *her* Donald and held *him* close. And Mrs MacLeod snatched up *her* Donald and held *him* close. They looked at one another. They looked around at the other villagers and they looked at their baby Donalds – they all looked exactly the same! What were they going to do? How were they going to tell them apart? What would happen if they got them mixed up and they took the wrong Donald home?

'Now what are we going to do?' they said.

For a long time there was silence as the villagers thought and thought and thought.

At last, an old man said, 'We don't know what to do, but what if you went up the hill to the old, wise woman. Maybe she could help.'

In those days every village had an old, wise woman.

'Oh yes! We will go up the hill to the old, wise woman,' said the young parents. So, the MacCraes, the MacLennans and the MacLeods and their three Donalds went up the hill to visit the old, wise woman.

But even before they had knocked, she opened the door.

'Oh yes,' she said, 'I've been expecting you. I've had the feeling in my bones that something unusual, something very unusual was going to happen in our village. Three . . . yes, three fine little boys . . . and all of them with red hair . . . and all of them with brown eyes, sparkling brown eyes . . . yes, this is unusual and they all look exactly the same. What will you call them?'

'Donald.'

'Donald.'

'Donald.'

'This is a wonder all right: three identical Donalds born in the same village at the same hour of the same day. However are you going to tell them apart?'

'That is why we came to you.'

'Oh yes,' she said, scratching her old, grey head. 'Well, well, I will have to think about this. Ahhh, but now it is getting late. Take the little ones home. By the morning you will be able to tell one Donald from the other. I tell you by sunrise tomorrow, you will be able to tell the one from the other. So take yourselves down the hill and put the little ones to sleep for the night.'

So the MacCraes, the MacLennans and the MacLeods set off down the hill. They kissed three Donalds goodnight and tucked them into three cradles. And they themselves went off to sleep. But the old, wise woman was wide awake and she was thinking.

As her fire crackled, she thought . . . And then at length she rose and went into the ben room, the room to the west of her little cottage where the evening sun shimmered from the ocean; red, gold, orange, out of a blue sky.

It was a room full of secrets and wonders. From floor to ceiling there were shelves; shelves full of wonders, boxes and bottles and jars full of secrets.

She looked around and, thinking of Donald MacCrae growing up in his sparkling cottage high on the hill, she reached up and pulled down a great jar. And she took off the lid. It was a jar in which she kept the colours of the sky and rainbow.

She reached in and pulled out a long strand of red, and she laid that on her ancient loom. She reached in and pulled out long strands of blue and strands of gold. And with these, the colours of the rainbow, she began to weave – over and under and under and over, over and under and under and over she wove.

And the moon rose into the night sky.

When she was finished weaving her gift for Donald MacCrae, she took it from the loom and laid it aside.

And she thought of Donald MacLennan, of the snug little cottage in the glen and of his father and mother working the land. Thinking of them, she reached up and pulled down from a shelf a jar filled with colours from the earth. And from it she took green of grass, red of rowan and yellow of broom. And with these, the colours of the earth, she began to weave – over and under and under and over, over and under and under and over she wove.

And the moon moved silently through the night sky.

When she finished weaving her gift for Donald MacLennan, she took it from her loom and laid it aside.

And she thought of Donald MacLeod sleeping in his sea-sprayed cottage by the shore and of his father, the fisherman. She reached up and pulled down from a shelf a

jar filled with colours from the sea. She took the dark blue of the deep ocean and the green of the dulse, the seaweed, and she took yellow and red from the sunsets dancing on the water. With these, the colours of the sea, she began to weave – over and under and under and over, over and under and under and over she wove.

And the moon was sinking in the west.

At length she finished and she took her gift for Donald MacLeod from the loom. Now she was ready. Carefully, she folded her three gifts over her arm, came out into the night and hurried down the hill. The moon was sitting like a great silver ball right on top of the dark, blue sea. And she climbed the hill to the home of the MacCraes.

In these days no one locked their doors so, without knocking, she slipped quietly inside. And there in a shaft of moonlight she saw the little white bundle with tufts of red hair sleeping peacefully in the cradle. She wrapped Donald MacCrae in the colours of the rainbow and crept out, down the hill and up the glen to the home of the MacLennans.

She opened the door and went in, and there – another moonlit bundle with tufts of red hair. She wrapped Donald MacLennan in the colours of the earth, slipped out and made her way down, down, down to the foot of the glen to the seashore home of the MacLeods.

And the moon was a silvery fingernail above the horizon.

Inside the cottage was one last little bundle of white

with tufts of red hair, sleeping in his cradle. She wrapped Donald MacLeod in the colours of the sea, softly closed the door and came back up the hill to her own cottage.

The moon sank into the sea, and in the east, above the tree-covered mountains, the sun burst with red and yellow and pink and gold and wakened the whole green glen.

In the village, three bright pairs of sparkling brown eyes awoke and three hungry red mouths opened to welcome the day. Three sleepy couples rose and went to them. There they found the gifts of the old, wise woman.

They wanted to show everyone, so they gathered up their little bright bundles and took them out.

Under the rowan tree and in the light of the morning, the villagers gathered.

There was Donald MacCrae wrapped in the colours of the rainbow, Donald MacLennan wrapped in the colours of the earth and Donald MacLeod wrapped in the colours of the sea. Now they could easily tell one Donald from the other. And word spread throughout the village.

Word spread over the mountains and into the glens, into far parts of the land to other families and clans, and everyone heard of those beautiful gifts.

'We would like colours and patterns for our families,' the people said.

And so it was that the old, wise woman taught the people how to weave the colours of the sky and of the earth and of the sea. And every family got its own colours and its own patterns.

And there are those who say that it is because of these three remarkable Donalds, and the old, wise woman's gifts, that tartan came to Scotland!

Selected titles also available from
SCOTTISH CHILDREN'S PRESS

An A–Z of Scots Words for young readers
1 899827 03 X

Aiken Drum: a story in Scots for young readers
Anne Forsyth; illustrated by Dianne Sutherland; 1 899827 00 5

Bobby Boat and the Big Catch: an Aberdeen Adventure
Thomas Chalmers; illustrated by Billy Dobbie; 1 899827 54 4

Bobby Boat in Trouble at Sea: an Oban Adventure
Thomas Chalmers; illustrated by Billy Dobbie; 1 899827 55 2

Classic Children's Games from Scotland
Kendric Ross; illustrated by John MacKay; 1 899827 12 9

Kitty Bairdie: a story in Scots for young readers
Anne Forsyth; illustrated by Dianne Sutherland; 1 899827 01 3

Sandy MacStovie's Monster
Moira Miller; illustrated by Rob Dee; 1 899827 27 7

Teach the Bairns to Bake: Traditional Scottish Baking for Beginners
Liz Ashworth; 1 899827 24 2

Teach the Bairns to Cook: Traditional Scottish Recipes for Beginners
Liz Ashworth; 1 899827 23 4

Wallace, Bruce, and the War of Independence
Antony Kamm; illustrated by Jennifer Campbell; 1 899827 15 3

Wee Willie Winkie and other rhymes for Scots children
Fiona Petersen (ed.); 1 899827 17 X

When I Wear My Leopard Hat: poems for young children
Dilys Rose; illustrated by Gill Allan; 1 899827 70 6

The Wild Haggis an the Greetin-faced Nyaff
Stuart McHardy; illustrated by Alistair Phimister; 1 899827 04 8

for further information on these or any of our other titles,
please contact **SCOTTISH CHILDREN'S PRESS**, Unit 14,
Leith Walk Business Centre, 130 Leith Walk, Edinburgh EH6 5DT